and   s

The Ghostly Rider

and Other Chilling Stories

Hernán Moreno-Hinojosa

PIÑATA
BOOKS

PIÑATA BOOKS
ARTE PÚBLICO PRESS
HOUSTON, TEXAS

This volume is made possible through grants from the City of Houston through The Cultural Arts Council of Houston, Harris County.

Piñata Books are full of surprises!

Arte Público Press
University of Houston
452 Cullen Performance Hall
Houston, Texas 77204-2004

Cover illustration and design by Giovanni Mora

Moreno-Hinojosa, Hernán
    The Ghostly Rider and Other Chilling Stories / by Hernán Moreno-Hinojosa.
        p.   cm.
    Summary: A collection of twelve traditional tales from southern Texas viewed through the author's experiences on the cattle ranches owned by his father, including one in an area known as "el desierto muerto."
    Contents: Lady death—Sometimes they come back—God works in mysterious ways—The ghostly rider—The vanishing hitchhiker—The light out yonder—Astronomical odds—The little girl who could see death—Belia—The year of the witch—Last is not so bad—The shape-shifting jackass.
    ISBN 1-55885-400-2
    1. Tales—Texas. [1. Folklore—Texas. 2. Ranch life—Texas.] I. Title.
PZ8.1.M797Gh   2003
398.2′09764′05—dc21   2003049836
                                               CIP

3 4 5 6 7 8 9 0 1 2   10 9 8 7 6 5 4 3 2 1

To my wife, Linda, who makes all things seem possible . . .
To Tío Juan Rodríguez, protagonist of "Sometimes They
Come Back" and "The Shape-shifting Jackass."

Table of Contents

Foreword

A long, long time ago, before radio and television revolutionized entertainment, the oral tradition of storytelling predominated. Tales handed down by word of mouth by *la gente mayor—los abuelos, los tíos, las tías*—told artfully around a fireplace, or by a roaring campfire late at night, were what the close-knit family looked forward to after a hard day's work.

I grew up in rural South Texas during a time when this tradition was already dying and radio and television were beginning to flourish. Nonetheless, I learned to love *cuentos*, tales of *espantos* told by wise old-timers whose era was rapidly coming to a close. These tales, old when our grandparents first heard them, never failed to spark the imagination. For example, who can ever forget the classic Mexican folktale of La Llorona—The Weeping Woman, a chilling tale that also offers a social lesson that should not be ignored? Who is not moved by the story of this poor woman who drowned her own children in order to exact revenge against the lover who returned to his wife? For her crime, La Llorona is condemned to lament the death of her children near the site of their demise. People still speak of La Llorona, who will eternally walk in a twilight realm, a dim, mysterious nether region that lies between the world of the living and the world of the dead.

What follows are just a few of my favorite *cuentos*. These are stories of ghosts, spook lights, and people who practice magic. These are stories of unnatural creatures, monsters if you will, that cannot exist, yet somehow seem to.

I sincerely hope that you will enjoy these collected stories as much as I have. However, before I leave you to your book, a single cautionary note. Please do not read these stories aloud, around a campfire late at night, in the presence of very young children. Enjoy!

Acknowledgments

There are so many people to thank. The marvelous people of South Texas who selflessly shared their knowledge and stories that should not be forgotten. All who contributed information, shared stories, proofread the raw manuscript and offered advice. The talented members of the West Oaks Writer's Group who put up with me, encouraged me, and critiqued my work. Oscar García who shared his own story.

In a very special way, Mr. Doug Briggs of Alief, Texas, who believed in this manuscript and who encouraged me and offered expert advice and direction. My wife Herlinda, who makes all things seem possible. Mr. Francis Gutowski, my brilliant friend who was able to explain to me, a simple man, in simple terms, what *time* is. My brother Eliazar, who came forth with a story from his youth that otherwise might have been lost. Of course, Melly Rodríguez, Tío Juan, Felix, Lili, Alma, Alex, Hector, Sue, Martha, Clovis, Russ, Renée, and Carmen all deserve thanks. You know who you are. Inadvertently, someone is always forgotten. For this I do apologize and if you will please remind me, I will be sure to acknowledge you the next time!

Lady Death

L a Florida was a working horse and cattle ranch situated right in the middle of what was known as *el desierto muerto* back in the days when the Nueces River, rather than the Rio Grande, delineated the border between Texas and Old Mexico. In spite of the region, La Florida Ranch flourished and in later years provided employment for enough families that a one-room schoolhouse was established for the children of the laborers.

In those days Tío Nieves Hinojosa was a young man, carefree and sometimes reckless by his own account. Every evening after work, the men gathered around at the ranch store to enjoy a cold beer. They sat on the spacious, covered wooden store porch and swapped stories: "Did you hear how a yearling bull dragged Hernándo over at Ranchito María? He is going to be plucking grass burrs from his long johns for the next two weeks!"

"Roel finally broke that sorrel mare that threw Polo, who said that no *caballo* could throw him. He was right. That sorrel is a *yegua*, not a *caballo*!"

An old man was always there with the cowboys, sitting in an old rocking chair. His legs were covered by an old blanket and his .30 caliber Winchester-Center-Fire carbine always rested on his lap. Nieves wondered about this enigmatic figure, this old-timer known to all as José the invalid.

People said that José became an invalid one day after seeing an apparition that frightened him badly. With no one around to give him *agua con azúcar*—water laced with sugar to overcome the fright—José never quite recovered. Psychiatrists today would probably classify his condition as post-traumatic stress syndrome, but back then people said *que había quedado asustado*—that he remained frightened or traumatized. The man had been wasting away for years with no apparent remedy for his present condition. People said that the old man had come face-to-face with death itself.

Nieves knew the story that circulated about José, but he wanted to hear firsthand from the old-timer about the circumstances which led to his present condition. In those days people respected their elders, and Nieves was no exception. However, Nieves admitted that he had been drinking when he struck up a conversation with the old-timer.

"José," Nieves began, "tell me, why do you waste your time sitting on that rocker? I was thinking that you and I could jump on my horse and ride off to the dance." Taking the lead with an imaginary partner, Nieves executed a quick two-step, stomping loudly on the wooden porch with his cowboy boots.

The old man cracked a tiny smile as if the idea of

attending a dance appealed to him. Or perhaps he was recalling better times and faded love.

"I am no good on the dance floor anymore, Nieves. I leave that to younger men such as you, but in my day," the old man smiled broadly, "I danced with the prettiest *señoritas* in all of La Florida."

Nieves bought the old man a beer and sat on the porch next to him. "José," Nieves began once more, "for as long as I have known you, all you do is sit in that old rocker all day long."

"It is true, Nieves, since I saw that *maldita mujer* I have been useless. That cursed woman is to blame."

"What cursed woman, José?" Nieves inquired earnestly. "An old love, perhaps—"

The old man's spontaneous outburst of laughter cut Nieves off in mid-sentence. "No, Nieves, that was not an old love, it was *la muerte.*" The old man doffed his hat, quickly making the sign of the cross. "It was Death herself!"

"I am curious now, José." Nieves took a quick swig from his long-necked bottle. "Why don't you tell me the whole story?"

"You are too young, Nieves," the old man protested, "you will be frightened."

Now it was Nieves' turn to laugh, "Frightened? Fear is for women and for cowards. I am neither. I am a man, and your story will not frighten me."

The old man was silent for a moment. Both men stared

at the buzzard that had come to light on a fence post in front of the store.

Then the old man, perhaps convinced that Nieves should learn something about fear, began to tell his story:

"The sun was going down that day, Nieves. We were through working the fields when I started back alone, leaving the rest of the men to load the tools. I walked but a little distance when I noticed a woman standing in the meadow looking at me.

"I stopped and looked back at her. Her face was not distinguishable in the fading light of day. She appeared young and attractive if a little tall, at least taller than the local girls. She wore a black dress that seemed decorated with large disks, like silver dollars that shone brilliantly in the fading light. By her form and dress I did not recognize her, but a lot of *gitanos*—gypsies—traveled through town in those days."

The old man paused to take a swig from his bottle of beer. He sighed and looked into the distance before continuing.

"I started toward the woman to see if perhaps she had become separated from her caravan and needed help. As soon as I started toward her, she turned and started walking away. I hurried up a bit to catch up to her. When I was closer she stopped and said to me over her shoulder, '*Sigueme que te hare feliz*—follow me, for I shall make you happy.'

"Before I could react to her invitation, I noticed her feet. They were not touching the ground. Now she was facing me. I looked up to find myself staring into a face devoid of flesh, the face of Death herself! That is why, Nieves, you now find me here, wasting away in this rocking chair."

Nieves was silent for a moment, perhaps appraising the old man's story. "You are telling me, José," Nieves inquired, "that a woman frightened you, rendering you useless?"

"*Sí*, Nieves," the old man affirmed with conviction, "she was *la muerte.*"

Nieves rose rapidly, unable to conceal his disdain. "How I wish, José," Nieves spoke with much bravado, "that your woman had appeared to me. I would have extended my hand to her, that she could ride *en ancas*—behind me on my horse. I, for one, know how to show a woman a good time, José."

The old man continued in a somber tone. "Nieves, you don't know what you say. Her face, it was horrible! It was Death's face, a flesh-less skull with glowing red embers where her eyes should be."

"Nevertheless," Nieves insisted, emphasizing each syllable, "no woman frightens me! For someone to frighten me, that person would have to be more of a man than I am."

Just then Nieves caught sight of José's Winchester resting on his lap. "And that big Winchester, José, what do you need that for?"

"One never knows, Nieves. It could come in handy—"

"Handy? Handy for what?" Nieves interrupted sarcastically. "Can you even shoot it?"

"Why, in my day, Nieves, I would never miss a single shot with this Winchester."

"See that buzzard?" Nieves said pointing. "I will give you this silver dollar if you can hit it, even at this close range."

Eager to vindicate himself, the old man brought the Winchester to his shoulder with a quickness that startled Nieves. José took careful aim at the buzzard still perched on the fence post a mere thirty yards away. Nieves knew that the old .30 caliber, Winchester-Center-Fire, the forerunner of the more modern .30-30 Winchester, was effective out to a hundred yards. A dollar was some two-days' wages, a lot of money to give the old man if his bullet flew true. The thunderous *kaboom!* of the big Winchester brought all the men rushing outside just in time to witness the buzzard sail gracefully away, more alive than ever before.

When Nieves finished laughing, the old man looked him right in the eye and said, "You shall see, Nieves. Tonight you must ride home right through that meadow where Lady Death showed her hideous face to me."

Nieves' laughter seemed tinged with just a hint of fear now, nerves really; for a real man fears nothing, not even Death herself, and so Nieves said, "I do hope I run into her tonight, José, that I may show her a good time."

"Of such hopes one must be careful, Nieves. The wise man is careful what he wishes for," José cautioned.

"Ha, Ha!" Nieves laughed in the old man's face, "I shall

give Lady Death your regards, old man!" Nieves jumped on his horse and rode away.

Riding home alone in the dark, the old man's tale was starting to trouble Nieves. Even though there was a full moon that night, the shadows seemed longer than usual and the stillness of the night was overbearing. He kept looking over his shoulder as he rode. The only sound was the clop, clop, clop of his horse trotting gracefully upon the sandy loam and the gentle snort that his horse occasionally uttered. Nieves felt the grip of his big Colt on his hip with a sweaty palm. As far as he knew, Colonel Sam Colt's great equalizer—the colt revolver that made all men equal—was useless against the fate that awaited all men at the trail's end. How he wished he had not teased the old man so mercilessly!

Soon the meadow that José had described came into view in the naked moonlight. Nieves lived past the meadow, just beyond an arroyo. He hesitated. His horse looked back and gave a tiny snort as if to ask, "Why are we stopping?"

Perched on his saddle, Nieves looked all around. There was nothing to be seen except for the long, foreboding shadows. Shadows everywhere and that confounded silence. No crickets chirping, no coyotes baying at the moon. Not even the occasional "moo" from the cows that had to be reposing in the field, chewing their cud.

Nieves paced his horse back and forth for a good half-hour before devising a plan. His horse knew the way home, Nieves reasoned. He would release the reins, lean down hugging his horse's neck, close his eyes and not reopen them until he had traveled long enough to be past the haunted meadow. Yes, that was it. He would not reopen his eyes until he crossed the gully.

When Nieves figured he had ridden past the haunted grounds, he opened his eyes and sat up in his saddle. He smiled broadly. His plan had worked, the meadow was now behind him! Still smiling he started turning to glimpse at the haunted meadow behind him. As he turned, he caught sight of a woman with a flesh-less skull riding behind him! He crouched down in his saddle and spurred his horse on. The horse whined and sped rapidly along.

Surely, he thought, I've left it behind. But as he started to turn he saw the grinning skull right behind. "*¡Traigo a la muerte en ancas!*—That accursed woman is riding behind me on my own horse!" He spurred his horse on, even faster, until at long last he arrived at his ranch house. His brother came out with a kerosene lantern.

"Nieves, you are late again," his brother admonished. "We have much work to do in the morning."

"Yes," Nieves agreed, nervously looking all around.

"What is that?" His brother asked, pointing at something that dangled from his hat.

Nieves jerked his hat off. A piece of dried twig dangled

on a spiderweb from the side of his hat. He must have collected that as he rode blindly through the arroyo. Feeling very foolish, Nieves realized that it was the twig dangling from his hat that had frightened him. He figured that as he started to turn, his vision focused on the offending twig and his wild imaginings turned the twig into nothing less than Lady Death's grinning skull!

Sometimes They Come Back

People around La Colonia el Gato near San Juan, Texas, were already talking about how that Rodríguez boy had died. "It is such a shame," they whispered, "he was only eleven."

"And think of Cecilia, his poor mother," another voice would start, "how she suffers. He was only trying to earn a few coins to help the family out." They were not aware that sometimes . . . *they come back* . . .

The chain of events that led to Juan Rodríguez's untimely demise began two weeks earlier, when he was hired by Doña Tiburcia, the widowed lady who lived down the street from the Rodríguez residence. Doña Tiburcia lived in an old house with a cane-thatched roof. She was in her early forties and had become a widow at the age of thirty, when her husband was felled by a Carranzista bullet. Doña Tiburcia had no children of her own, but she was kind to her neighbor's children.

Doña Tiburcia kept hens and sold fresh farm eggs, thus earning enough money to lead a comfortable life. She was having trouble with one of her young hens. It was a wily, smallish, chocolate-colored chicken that would come around during feeding time but would disappear when it came time to lay her eggs. Doña Tiburcia tired of trying to find where her hen was disappearing to and asked Juan Rodríguez, then eleven years old, to help her find the hen.

"Juan," she asked, "see that chocolate-colored hen?"

"*Sí*, Doña Tiburcia," Juan acknowledged politely.

"Juan, that wily hen has concealed her nest from me. I am losing money from her production of eggs." Exasperation clearly showed in her voice as she spoke. "If you follow that little hen for me this morning and find her nest, I will pay you fifty cents."

Juan's face lit up. Fifty cents was a lot of money, and Juan knew that his family could really use it. There should be a nickel or two left over for Juan to spend as he would. Juan started watching the little chocolate-colored hen immediately.

The hen scratched the ground with the rest of the chickens before it started separating itself from the gaggle. It started making its way slowly, subtly toward the canal about a thousand feet from Doña Tiburcia's house. Juan followed the little hen at a distance. The hen reached the canal and walked a little way along one of the banks. Then the hen hesitated before a willow tree. The hen looked both ways, then taking a running start flew some six feet into the lower branches of the tree.

Juan snuck up the tree and soon spied the chicken's head bobbing from a hollow in one of the large branches. "Aha!" Juan said to himself. "So that is where the hen has been laying her eggs."

Juan returned to Doña Tiburcia who was amazed to learn that her hen had wandered so far from the henhouse. Nonetheless, they acquired a ladder and Juan caught the hen and recovered the eggs for Doña Tiburcia. Juan happily went home with fifty cents in his pocket while Doña Tiburcia sought out Don Pascual, the local handyman, to build a chicken coop for the little chocolate hen.

But the little chocolate hen refused to remain in the new coop. It would always manage to get out of the coop and wander off to lay her eggs out of its owner's reach. Doña Tiburcia reasoned that it was time to once again hire Juan. Doña Tiburcia was perhaps too kind; a lesser person surely would have prepared *caldo de pollo*—chicken soup—by this time.

"Juan," said Doña Tiburcia early the following morning, "I will pay you well to catch that wily chicken for me. It will not be easy, but you are young and spry enough to run it down on foot for me. Catch that little chicken for me, and I will give you two silver dollars."

"*Sí*, Doña Tiburcia," Juan answered with much enthusiasm. "I will catch that chicken for you even if it takes me all day."

Juan started pursuing the chicken at about ten o'clock

that morning. As quick as he was, Juan was not enjoying much success. The little chicken was even quicker, and wily as the devil himself, but Juan was determined to earn the two silver dollars for his family. An honest day's work, little Juan's father always said, never hurts anyone.

About four o'clock in the afternoon Juan suddenly realized that he was very thirsty. Politely he knocked on Doña Tiburcia's door and asked for a glass of water. Doña Tiburcia promptly brought Juan a big glass of cold water. Juan gulped the water down quickly and went outside, but suddenly he felt very dizzy. He leaned on the corner of the house for a moment. Not feeling well, Juan stumbled home. Soon Juan felt his eyesight failing him.

"Mamá," Juan cried out, stumbling into his own home. "Mamá, I cannot see and I am very dizzy."

"What is wrong, Juan?" his mother implored. "What has happened to you, *m'ijo*?"

"I don't know," Juan replied. "I drank a glass of water and now I can't see and I'm very dizzy."

Cecilia held her son as his face contorted, pushing his entire mouth to one side. Juan was now going into convulsions and his eyes were rolling into the back of his head.

Juan's mother quickly sent for Doña Juanita, the local midwife and *curandera*. This was 1933; even if a doctor could be found, there would be no money to pay for his services.

Doña Juanita soon arrived at the Rodríguez's house. "It is not good, Mrs. Rodríguez," the *curandera* announced.

"The boy has been struck with paralysis. He will not take any of the herbal remedies I have. I am afraid he will die."

Grief stricken, Juan's mother held her son all through the night. At about ten in the morning Juan stopped breathing. He became stiff and unresponsive. The grieving mother called for her sister.

"Cecilia," Juan's aunt said, "it is time to let the boy go. He is in a better place now. There are arrangements to be made . . ."

That night a wake was held in the Rodríguez's house for Juan. The following morning Juan's father went out to find someone to build a casket for their young son.

Juan's mother was alone in the house with her dead son. There was food to prepare for those who would attend the funeral that very afternoon.

"Mamá," a voice called from the bedroom. "Mamá, I can see!"

"Juan?" his mother inquired incredulously. "Juan, how can it be?"

"Mamá," Juan called cheerfully, "I can see the light of day!"

Awestruck, Mrs. Rodríguez stared at her son with disbelief. "But my son, how can this be? You were dead! Your father is out hiring someone to build a coffin for your funeral."

"Mamá," Juan replied with a child's innocence, "I didn't know that I was dead."

God Works in Mysterious Ways

Father Trino was a novice priest assigned to the Diocese of Guadalajara in Jalisco, Mexico. Novice priests were required to take turns manning the confessional during the noon hours, roughly between 11:00 a.m. and 1:00 p.m., during the week. By all accounts this was a taxing assignment in that it was extremely boring, as no one seemed willing to sacrifice their lunch hour to attend confession. Still, on the outside chance that some poor soul should require the Sacrament of Reconciliation, the pastor of the church insisted that a priest be available to minister to their needs. This was an excellent opportunity for a new priest to practice the virtue of patience, as two hours in the abandoned church sitting in the confines of the confessional seemed to drag on forever.

The church in Jalisco was an ancient structure, grandiose and elegant. The church was built of stone and tile with long corridors that led from the entrance steps and busy streets outside to the very back of the church where the confessional was situated.

Time passed slowly in the confessional, far from the

main entrance, seemingly a world away from the noisy, busy streets of the city of Jalisco. Father Trino sat quietly in his side of the confessional, patiently waiting, waiting. . . . Father Trino was certain that he must have dozed off when he sensed a presence on the other side of the confessional. The sensation that Father Trino experienced was so acute that he wondered how it could be possible for someone to walk up the tiled corridor without being heard. Before he could react, a woman's voice calling softly startled Father Trino.

"*Padrecito*," the woman pleaded, "will you hear my confession?"

Father Trino, overcome with surprise, quickly cleared his throat to hide his astonishment. "Of course, my child, that is why I am here."

"Thank you, Father," the woman replied, and proceeded to make her confession. "Bless me, Father, for I have sinned."

After the woman made her confession and offered her Act of Contrition, Father Trino blessed her, granting her absolution. The relief was plain in the woman's voice as she thanked him for the Sacrament of Reconciliation.

Father Trino smiled, his vigil had not been in vain and now his time in the confessional was coming to an end. He decided to peek out of the confessional to see how the woman had managed to walk so soundlessly upon the hard, cold tile floor. He would not recognize the woman since her back would be to him, so there would be no breach of confidence. Father Trino reasoned that the lady must have removed her shoes prior to entering the church and he merely wanted to confirm this. Before Father Trino could look outside, another woman's voice called to him from the penitent's side of the confessional. Now Father Trino was doubly puzzled. Was this something new? Penitents most certainly were *not* required to remove their shoes prior to entering the house of God. Still, he reasoned, his hearing should be acute enough to detect the slapping of bare feet on the hard tile floor, so what was happening?

It did not matter, another soul required his priestly services and he was only too happy to comply. "Yes, my child?"

"Father," the second lady inquired, "will you hear my confession?"

"Of course, my child."

After the Act of Contrition, Father Trino granted the second woman absolution. The woman, greatly relieved, thanked Father Trino and took her leave.

Now Father Trino was really listening for the patter of feet, bare or otherwise, down the long tiled corridors. No sound came. Certain that the penitent would have her back to him he quickly opened the door. Father Trino knew that even at a dead run no one could reach the front door in the time that had elapsed. Yet, to his astonishment, the corridors were deserted!

Father Trino caught his breath, and then rushed toward the front door acutely aware of the sound of his own footsteps echoing loudly in the deserted corridors of the church. When he reached the front door, Father Trino noticed that the door opened and that the smiling priest that had come to relieve him entered.

"Brother," Father Trino grasped the other priest by the shoulders, "two young women, did you see them exit the church as you came up the stairs?"

The relief priest seemed puzzled. "Nobody exited the church, Brother Trino, nor was anyone on the sidewalk as I came in."

Father Trino was greatly troubled by this announcement. He related the events of moments before to the relief priest.

The relief priest was much older, and had been at the Jalisco church for some years. He listened patiently to the novice priest's story, and then he offered this explanation:

"Father Trino," the older priest began, "people here say that about twenty years ago, two young ladies who were hurrying to this very church were struck down by a taxicab out front as they hastily crossed the street." The priest gestured toward the street. "It is believed that the two young ladies were on their way to confession when they were killed by the taxicab." Both men looked at each other for a moment. "The young ladies," the older priest continued, "never made it." His voice drifted away, ". . . until *now*. After all, Brother Trino, God does work in mysterious ways."

The Ghostly Rider

L ack of work in the fifties forced many Mexican-American families to leave the citrus groves of the Rio Grande Valley of Texas and move west, looking for work. Roberto Rodríguez and his family ended up in the City of Angels where Roberto was fortunate enough to find work in one of the factories.

Roberto liked this work far better than going from *el Valle* to *el Norte* to pick pole beans, strawberries, and cherries. The work at the factory was hard, but steady, and punching a time card was an efficient way to keep track of his hours and not be cheated on his pay. Roberto, barely out of his teens at the time, had been in Los Angeles six months. Soon, he realized, he would be able to buy his own car. For now, public transportation was the most practical way for Roberto to get around Los Angeles.

That Friday, for reasons that he cannot really explain, Roberto got off to an early start, catching an earlier bus that traveled his usual route to work. Roberto sat in the half-empty bus dreaming of better times to come and watching people board and exit every block or so. Suddenly, Roberto noticed a most attractive young lady standing in the bus aisle.

The girl was petite, with luscious black hair, big beautiful brown eyes and was lightly tanned by the California sun. She couldn't be more than nineteen or twenty years old. When did that lovely lady board the bus? The two made eye contact and the girl flashed a smile at Roberto. To his delight, the girl walked up to Roberto and asked if the seat next to him was taken. Roberto, unable to find his voice, quickly scooted over and motioned for the girl to sit next to him.

The girl was as charming as she was beautiful, and Roberto lost all track of time engaged in conversation with her. Suddenly, the girl realized that she had missed her stop a few blocks back, so Roberto gallantly volunteered to walk her home.

Walking back to her apartment, the girl told Roberto that she was cold. Ever the gentleman, he promptly removed his leather jacket and draped it across the girl's shoulders. Holding the jacket close, the girl smiled and thanked Roberto for his gallantry.

Once at the girl's front door the couple engaged in conversation for another half hour or so. Finally the girl told Roberto that he was going to be late to work. He glanced at his watch and realized that he had to hurry in order to make it to work on time. Realizing that he did not even know the girl's name and that now he must rush off, Roberto blurted out, "What's your name, can I see you again?"

The girl smiled and answered, "My name is Marta, and now you must hurry so you won't be late to work."

The couple kissed and Roberto turned to catch the next Metro bus. Marta called out to Roberto to get his jacket, but he yelled back over his shoulder that he would return for it on Monday.

The following Monday, Roberto, eager to see the beautiful young lady again, left home early to stop for his jacket. The girl's father answered the door.

"Sir," Roberto asked politely, "*¿Está Marta?*—Is Marta home?"

"*¿Marta?*" The man inquired with some curiosity.

"Yes, I loaned her my jacket on Friday, and she said that I could pick it up today."

"Young man," the older man replied somberly, "you must be at the wrong apartment."

"*¿Marta no vive aquí?*—Marta doesn't live here?"

"I had a daughter named Marta, she died some years ago. You must be looking for a different Marta."

Stunned, Roberto replied, "But sir, this was the apartment and the door where I dropped Marta off last Friday. I'm sure of it!"

Moved by Roberto's sincerity, the older man said, "The graveyard is not far from here, son. Would you like to see her grave? I take her flowers every Friday."

Together, the man and Roberto walked to the graveyard. On a grassy knoll, beneath a weeping willow stood a single grave. As Roberto knelt by the grave with the old man,

Roberto read the inscription on her tombstone:

Marta González
1925-1945

RIP

There, draped across the back of Marta's tombstone, Roberto found his black leather jacket.

The Vanishing Hitchhiker

I was a little girl then and we were living in Mission, Texas. My dad one day said, "Sue, let's go see Grandpa Leftie."

We called Grandpa "leftie" because he lost his left arm in the war. He almost bled to death, and later was honorably discharged with a Purple Heart Medal. His grandchildren affectionately called him "Grandpa Leftie" because he was *left* with only one arm. Grandpa lived in Pharr, Texas, and I always enjoyed making the drive from Mission to Pharr with my dad.

In those days there was not the heavy flow of traffic on the highways that we see today. Country drives were slow-paced and pleasant then. In good weather the car windows remained open and the old AM radios, which were not dependable on the open road between cities, remained off. It was a time when people could enjoy the fresh country air and spend quality time with one another.

We had not traveled far, as we had not been on the road for more than a few minutes, when my dad pointed out a man soliciting a ride near a crossroad. As we neared and the hitchhiker came into view, we realized that he seemed familiar. Why, it was an old shirttail cousin of ours. He always stood there asking for a ride.

My dad pulled the car over onto the soft road shoulder and stopped in front of my cousin. As my hitchhiking cousin hurried over, Dad called out, "Hey, Eddie, hop in. We're on our way to Pharr to see Grandpa Leftie."

Eddie walked past me to the back door, opened the car door, and got in. I heard the door slam shut and we drove off.

"Eddie," Dad asked, "how have you been? We haven't seen you in some time. Where do you want us to drop you off?"

There was no reply.

"Eddie?" Dad asked, starting to look back.

I turned all the way around in my seat and looked the entire rear seat over. I even leaned over and looked into the floorboard of the car. Eddie was *not* in the car. I looked helplessly at dad. I was so sure Eddie had gotten into the back seat.

"Sue," Dad said to me, "maybe he just changed his mind—"

"But Daddy," I protested, "I heard Eddie open and close the door. I am *sure* he got into the back seat."

"Honey," Dad continued, "maybe he didn't want to go as far as Pharr. People are always giving Eddie rides. He just decided to wait for someone else to come along."

We talked about going back to see why he didn't get in,

but those were simpler times then. On open country roads in the valley, between small towns, people hitched rides all the time. There was not so much malice in the world then, and we did not really fear for his safety.

"Besides," my dad reasoned, "Eddie is all grown-up. He is a man, he can take care of himself, and he can certainly decide who he wants to catch a ride with."

The rest of the trip to Pharr was completely uneventful. It was just a pleasant country drive with Dad to see Grandpa.

At Grandpa's house, after greeting everyone present, we settled in the living room to talk.

"What's new, son?" Grandpa inquired.

"Oh, I almost forgot—we stopped to give Eddie a ride down by the crossroads where he always hitches rides—"

"Cousin Eddie?" Grandpa asked.

"Yeah, Cousin Eddie, but he didn't get in. I guess," Dad continued, "he decided he didn't want to come all the way to Pharr."

"You're not the only one who has been giving Cousin Eddie rides," Grandpa said somberly. "Eddie is still out there hitching rides, even though he died five months ago."

The Light Out Yonder

Every Texan over the age of thirty has heard of the Marfa Ghost Lights, mysterious orbs of white light indigenous to the desert region of West Texas, close to Marfa, Texas. However, who has ever heard of the South Texas Spook Lights, a tale repeated in oral tradition since my family settled in South Texas around 1806?

Old-timers had a name for this anomaly. They called it *la luz del llano*. Literally the light of the prairie, this expression was used to name an ominous ball of light seen "out yonder," when most of South Texas open land consisted of grassy meadows.

As a child, I delighted in listening to my parents tell of their encounters with *la luz del llano*. "I would often see it," Dad would begin in a somber tone, "when I rode home alone late at night. The first few times it gave me quite a start. I thought that it might be a bad man waiting for a chance to rob me. After a while I realized that the light didn't seem to startle my horse." Then he smiled, "Animals have good instincts about this sort of thing, so I stopped worrying about it."

"Once," Mom added, "it almost came in through the kitchen window, nearly scaring all the women silly."

Dad laughed as Mom hit him on the shoulder playfully.

In those days people generally accepted that the lights were the souls of people murdered by bandits, or massacred by Indians. An interesting variation of this story was that the lights marked the place where a murdered person had buried treasure, just before dying. An old man whom all the youngsters called Tío Manuel supposedly recovered a lot of treasure over a period of several years. It was even said that he had found, along with Spanish silver and gold coins, a knife fashioned entirely from gold.

His methods were simple and said to be tried and true. Although I never knew Tío Manuel to be in possession of more than a few folding dollars and I never did see the fabled gold knife, he was a drinking man who always seemed to have the means to support his vice. In his own way he was generous, allowing the widow lady next door to tap into his city water supply at no charge, and dispensing nickels and dimes to the neighboring kids for candy and soda pop.

Preparing for the treasure hunt was simple enough. This involved waiting for a full moon, having a grub hoe and a shovel handy, as well as a kerosene lantern and the prerequisite bottle of contraband tequila. When the hour was late, by the light of the moon, the treasure seeker would wander around and wait to spy the origin of the light. The more prudent treasure hunter would simply mark the spot, and then return the following night. The bolder one might begin digging immediately.

By the time I was old enough to be interested in such things, Tío Manuel didn't hunt treasures anymore. Some said that he had found enough silver and gold to last a lifetime. Others whispered that it was not so. That on one occasion Tío Manuel did not wait to dig the following night, as was his custom. On that night, when he had excavated a good sized hole in the sandy loam, a hole deep enough that he could not exit rapidly, a disembodied voice called to him from the darkness:

"*¿Qué buscas que no has perdido?*" the voice demanded. "What do you seek that you have not lost?"

After that, Tío Manuel was never the same. Early the following morning his friends found him, still in the hole with but a swallow of tequila left in his bottle. His kerosene lantern had burned dry and was long cold. He was dazed, dehydrated, and forever broken of his zeal to hunt for lost treasure. The general consensus was that Tío Manuel's rapidly deteriorating health was a direct result of that particular experience, and not his continuous, considerable consumption of alcohol. *¡Quién sabe!*

My own father was less adventurous and far more practical. He believed that *la luz del llano* was nothing more than an optical illusion, a mirage of sorts. He believed that the lights were real, but distant and somehow only seemed closer to the observer than they really were.

Once I asked him why he believed that they were merely illusory and I was surprised to learn that one night he actually chased one of the lights on horseback.

"You tried to catch it?" I asked in awe.

"Sure, but it always stayed the same distance ahead of my horse. If I sped up to a gallop, it sped up. If I slowed to a trot, it slowed down, always managing to keep the same distance between us. Soon I tired of this game and figured that it had to be an illusion, perhaps a reflection from the highway caused by passing cars."

From my father's explanation I could not reason how his account could be correct; by the time I heard this account there were no more *llanos*. The ranchlands that I was familiar with were covered with *nopal, mesquite, palo blanco,* and *huisache.* There was no way that *anything* could be seen from the distant highway! And hadn't the lights been around long before the automobile and the highways?

My father must have read the puzzled expression on my face because he smiled and said, "Tell you what, son. Tío Nieves will be here this weekend. Ask him to tell you about *la luz del llano.*"

Tío Nieves Hinojosa, my mother's oldest brother and my favorite uncle, was a gifted storyteller. I could sit for hours listening to him tell of his adventures on both sides of the border during his younger days. The week didn't go by fast enough as I waited for his big, gray New Yorker Chrysler to pull into our driveway.

Finally, that hot, lazy, dusty Saturday afternoon rolled

around in Hebbronville, Texas. That day, sitting through a fully colorized action movie at the ultra modern El Rancho Theater was not a viable option. For only twenty cents, one could lounge around in relative comfort on the red velvet seats and escape the oppressive afternoon heat in air conditioned comfort. El Rancho Theater was a haven from the heat and the dust in a time when few could afford air-conditioned cars, much less home air conditioning. No one really cared what was on the matinee, cowboys and Indians or some dull romantic drama, so long as we had the extra money for a delicious nickel bag of fresh popcorn. For the lucky few who could scrape up yet another nickel, a refreshingly cool, though never cold, cherry cola could be purchased from the vending machine in the lobby. But that Saturday none of that mattered. Tío Nieves would be in town and he would bring an action movie to my own living room with his vivid storytelling.

After dinner, sitting in our cool, spacious, brick and tile living room, I was able to corner my uncle and ask him about *la luz del llano*. It didn't take much prodding; he seemed to take as much delight in telling his tale as I in listening.

"It was late one fine autumn evening when I was riding home alone, that I noticed the spook light dancing about just ahead of me. As I sped my mount to catch up to it, the light, a white luminous orb about five inches in diameter, also sped up. I was more determined than ever to catch up to this mysterious, elusive will-o'-the-wisp, so I pushed my pony even harder. It was a good horse I rode, and he loved to run, but to my astonishment the light maintained a uniform distance ahead of me."

My uncle always seemed to know when to pause in his storytelling to keep his audience adequately in suspense. Now my uncle decided that he had to have a cup of coffee. He excused himself and made his way to the kitchen where he deliberately waited, making small talk to Mom as his coffee cooked. Then he dutifully thanked her for the coffee and ambled slowly back to the big, red easy chair in the living room. Now he pulled the small coffee table closer and after slowly settling back down, he continued his story.

Just when I thought I should give up the chase so as to not overexert my horse, the light seemed to fatigue. As I let my horse pace slowly back and forth, the light came to rest atop a fence post. I had been riding pretty hard after the light, so now I just let my pony catch his breath."

At that precise moment my uncle decided he couldn't live without a cigarette, so he sent me to fetch an ashtray. I hurried back with a large ashtray with the State of Texas recessed into a heavy porcelain block dyed turquoise and earth tones. Then my uncle fumbled through all his pockets looking for his cigarettes. It was only my love and respect for him that kept me from bursting out with "You know they are in your left vest pocket, just get them and get on with the story!"

My uncle lit a menthol flavored cigarette, took a puff, and then exhaled a long stream of blue-gray smoke before continuing. "I don't know how long I waited, exactly. It was perhaps ten or twenty minutes. When I was satisfied that easing forward would not alarm the spook light, I gently eased my mount onward. Well, wouldn't you know it?"

"What?" I asked, all wide-eyed and awed-struck.

"As I eased closer I was soon able to discern that the light was really nothing more than a rather large firefly."

"A firefly?" I gasped.

"Yes," my uncle replied, "all the hullabaloo about *la luz del llano* was over a harmless insect, so I left the light resting on the fence post and proceeded home." My uncle's somber expression never changed. If he was kidding, he never gave any indication.

Years later, as a teenager, I convinced myself that spook lights were nothing more than the fabrication of old-timers whose minds had perhaps been addled by too many hours in the sun. After all, these poor souls led a harsh existence, laboring hard to make an honest living. Now, in their golden years, they seemed to reminisce memories that I could not help but believe had been fabricated in order to justify otherwise uneventful lives. A tremendous conflict raged within me. This was the transitional period between the innocent child who accepts everything his elders say, and the enlightened teenager who must question everything. A part of me wanted wholeheartedly to believe and share the magic and know the awe that surely must accompany the appearance of an honest-to-goodness spook light. I wanted to believe; yet another part of me insisted that I was far too sophisticated to accept such nonsense. It was a time of flux for me, a time for change. A bittersweet time when so many things near and dear to the child in all of us are relinquished. A time to stop believing in fairy tales.

My father, bless his kind, knowing soul, offered his explanation:

"Son," he began, "when the Spaniards first came to South Texas, they found miles and miles of grassy flatlands. With them they brought horses and cattle. Both cattle and horses love to forage on the mesquite bean, but their digestive system has the curious inability to completely digest the seed. Wherever a horse or cow drops, a mesquite tree is planted. Eventually, son, the grassy meadows became a chaparral. In a similar fashion the cactus spreads. The meadows became choked with cactus and mesquite shrubbery. Cactus can be burned in the winter as fodder for cattle. Not so with mesquite. The mesquite just spreads, getting taller and denser until the ground is reclaimed through hard work with ax and grub hoe. *La luz del llano*, son, is a meadow light. The meadows are now overgrown with brush, so the light cannot be seen as readily. When the fields are cleared, the light will return. You will see."

For my father's sake I tried to feign good cheer. In fact I was sorely disappointed knowing that I would never be an eyewitness to this wondrous phenomena. I even felt belittled, expected to believe such an outlandish tale. I lacked my father's foresight to see that eventually the fields would have to be cleared, if for no other reason, to afford livestock their grazing rights.

Even so, there was no light, *la luz del llano* was a myth, and to me, that was the same thing as a lie.

Fresh out of high school I moved to the lower Rio Grande Valley of Texas. There I met another teenager who was to tell me a most interesting story.

Robert and I had much in common. We were both in our late teens, we worked together, and we were both avid hunters. Robert naturally assumed that I was from one of the numerous communities that make up *el Valle*. He was pleased to learn that I came from the brush country of Texas. He was even more pleased to learn that my family leased several hundred acres of fine, whitetail deer hunting land. When I told him that most of that acreage was in Jim Hogg County, his expression of delight fell away.

Robert seemed uneasy, a strange reaction since we were the best of friends. He looked around as if trying to decide if he could share some dark secret with me. Finally, he cracked a tiny smile and began to speak:

"Several years ago, when I was about fifteen, my older

brother Charlie leased some acreage for deer hunting in Jim Hogg County. After much coaxing I convinced him to let me hunt with him. Well, we didn't have a cabin or camper, so we pitched a big green tent my brother had bought at an army surplus store. That same afternoon my brother decided to go into Hebbronville. I volunteered to stay behind and guard our belongings. When he didn't return, I just fell asleep on a cot propped by the north wall of our tent.

"Around midnight, a bright light that shone right through the tent woke me up. I figured that my brother had returned and driven the car right up to the tent with the headlights on bright. So I just adjusted my sleeping bag to keep the cold out, rolled over, and went right back to sleep.

"Well, just before dawn I awoke alone in the tent. I thought that my brother must have gone on to hunt, taking the car with him. I shook the sleep from my head, dreading to leave my warm, cozy sleeping bag. Anxious to catch up to my brother, I got up and hurriedly dressed, grabbed my Winchester Model 70 .243 rifle, and hurried off to my blind.

"Outside, the stars against the vast expanse of black sky offered little light. The moon itself was but an orange sickle, so with my trusty two-cell Ray-O-Vac to light my way, I followed the old cow path leading to my blind.

"The predawn mist was clinging to the ground, swirling up like smoke, and lingering everywhere. Mesquite branches reached out from either side of the cow path to brush my shoulders with their dew-licked twigs. Soon I found myself walking up to a fence I would have to cross in order to reach my blind. I was momentarily stunned to see a strange light coming toward me from beyond the fence.

"As everyone knows, poachers are not uncommon in that area. My brother talked about finding poachers on his lease who fled the moment that he challenged them. So I figured the light must be a poacher carrying a lantern, coming my way. Boy, would my brother be proud and consider me all grown-up if I ran the poacher off for him.

"Well, I just killed my flashlight, stepped behind some brush, and waited. I reasoned that the poacher would reach the fence and set his lantern down, extinguish it, or simply raise it over the fence and lay it down on my side before attempting to cross the fence. That would put the trespasser at a distinct disadvantage. At least he would not have his rifle ready, and that would signal the perfect time for me to challenge him. I had the element of surprise on my side. I could see his light and he still didn't have any idea that I was around.

"Let me tell you, *nothing* could have prepared me for what happened next. Imagine my astonishment when the light did not even slow down approaching the fence. It didn't slow down, it didn't stop, and it didn't rise nor descend. *No one was carrying it!* It was a disembodied light coming right at me, moving of its own volition. It came right *through* the fence, and I won't lie to you, I lost all interest in hunting that day.

"I hurried back to our tent and stayed there until my

brother finally showed up sometime around noon. He said that the water pump had gone out on the car and he was forced to spend the night in Hebbronville, Texas."

Robert sighed and said, "Since then I've never returned to hunt in Jim Hogg County. Truth to tell, I don't believe I ever will."

Is the light still out there, laying low in the mesquite-choked plains of Jim Hogg County? Now I believe that there is some substance to the legend of *la luz del llano*. I believe that *la luz* waits for the root plow—an implement that is attached to a tractor and brush is cleared quickly and efficiently—to reclaim sufficient acreage to once again thrill the fortunate spectator with its nighttime dancing antics. If ever I do encounter this mysterious light when I have occasion to be in South Texas late at night, I know I will not be afraid. Whether the light turns out to be a "rather large firefly," or perhaps the soul of some person long ago murdered, my reaction shall be the same. I will welcome *la luz del llano* like an old friend, an old friend who has been gone too long!

Astronomical Odds

There was no thunder. Lightning did not light up the sky. The wind did not howl and moan. It was in fact *not* a dark and stormy night. It was merely dark, and except for the endless drone, buzzing and whining of the big motors, nothing stirred. All was still within the forty-acre chain-link enclosure of gray fiberglass tanks, beige steel-and-glass buildings, and massive concrete pads. I was glad to see Alex Pérez amble slowly into the control room of the El Mesquite Uranium Plant where I worked. He was coming in from the leach fields where he worked, monitoring wells and regulating flow into the plant.

The hour was late and we were both bone-weary from working the midnight shift all month long. Alex paused before the white Mr. Coffee machine. He knew he could depend on me to keep fresh coffee in the office during the graveyard shift. He poured a cup of coffee and added cream and sugar before settling down in one of the black office chairs.

Alex and I went back a long time and conversation was free and easy between the two of us. Although there never was a dearth of material to converse about, some nights just seemed to set the mood for conversation to turn, without warning or preamble, to matters of the great unknown. This was such a night.

"A few years ago," Alex started, "I drove a truck for Goodyear, delivering butane gas to all the customers outside of Hebbronville in Jim Hogg County. That day I was scheduled to make a delivery to Rancho Casa Redonda, off FM-1017 just past the Catholic Cemetery. Just a little ways in the main gate the road forked left and right, and I didn't know which way to go."

South Texas ranches could be quite large, sometimes expanding into neighboring counties and covering hundreds, if not thousands of acres. It was easy to appreciate Alex's dilemma. Turning a big truck around on a ranch road was not easy if you suddenly found yourself lost.

"So," I asked, "which fork did you take?"

"I couldn't decide, for all I knew the ranch was at least a few hundred acres. I didn't want to wander around for hours looking for a place to turn the truck around." Alex paused to sip his coffee.

"Fortunately, I noticed an old house near the dirt road. It was really a one-room shack with the old style cooking fireplace built right into the end of the house."

I could picture exactly what Alex was describing. The old fireplace had always been the most prominent feature of those old houses, one-room rectangular shacks made of weathered planks. I have always believed that the fireplace was built first. Then, almost as an afterthought, it was enclosed to provide a reprieve from the elements. Frequently one found the building completely destroyed, but the fireplace always remained sturdy and stable as if waiting for someone else to build a cabin around it.

"What caught my eye," Alex continued with a sad, solemn expression, "was a tiny wisp of white smoke billowing from the stone chimney stack. I realized someone had to be home as a fire would never be left unattended."

Alex sighed, rose laboriously from his chair to freshen his coffee, and continued his story. "I parked my truck on the side of the road and walked up to the shack to ask for directions. As I approached the door I could smell fresh *pan de campo* cooking inside. An old man, stooped with age and wearing regulation khaki work clothes came to the door, immediately inviting me for coffee and *pan de campo*."

The impromptu invitation was not unusual, and to decline such an offer without good reason was a serious breach of protocol. Because of the remoteness of their workstation and residence, ranch hands eagerly welcomed conversation and fellowship, even from strangers.

"It had been some time since I had any good shepherd coffee and country bread." Alex glimpsed balefully at the Styrofoam cup presently in his hand and added, "You know, we have been out of the cowboy business too long."

"Yep," I agreed, "cowboys ride four-wheelers now."

Alex added, "And they round up cattle with helicopters."

We looked at each other, silently appreciating the irony

of the modern West where a single whirlybird now did the work of a dozen cowboys on horseback. Perhaps the saddest thing of all was that the noble horse, the cowboy's constant companion, was all but displaced by the true iron horse, the steel pickup truck.

Alex nodded sadly and continued: "Anyway, more out of habit than anything else, I looked over my shoulder to see my truck safely off the side of the road. The day was so hot that heat waves emanating from the metal made the truck appear to wobble and undulate beneath the blazing sun. Satisfied that nothing was amiss I joined the old man indoors for some country bread and coffee. Afterwards I thanked him for his hospitality and asked him which fork to take to Rancho Casa Redonda headquarters. The old man nodded and told me to take the right fork, that I would see the main house just over the rise. I bade him good-bye and he bade me a *vaya con Dios*, and so I climbed back into my truck and went on to make my delivery.

"The name of the ranch, Casa Redonda, literally means 'round house'. The ranch was named for the main ranch house, which really was round. Apparently, the owner wanted a house that had no corners, so he built one made of brick and completely round.

"I arrived at the ranch and was filling up the butane tank when I struck up a conversation with the *caporal*, the ranch's foreman. As we waited we talked about the usual, how hot the days were and how dry the prairie was. I casually mentioned the old man who had given me directions, telling me which fork to take.

"The *caporal* gave me a funny look and asked, 'What old man?'

"'*El viejito*,' I answered, 'who lives in the shack by the road.'

"'There is just one old shack,' the *caporal* nodded as he spoke, 'with the big cooking fireplace, to the right of the main road.'

"'Sure,' I said, 'that's the one.'

"'No one lives there,' the *caporal* said abruptly. 'It has been abandoned for years.'

"'Nonsense,' I rationalized, 'there was smoke coming from the chimney, so I stopped to ask directions. The old man was cooking *pan de campo* and coffee—'

"'An old man did live there,' the *caporal* interrupted, 'about ten years ago.' Now the *caporal* turned and looked into the distance. He wiped the sweat off the back of his neck with a red bandanna. His tone told me that he was sincere. 'The old man died there, so no one goes near the shack anymore.' *The caporal* grinned, but the grin did not quite reach his eyes. 'Imagine,' he added nervously, 'they are afraid of him.' Now *el caporal* stopped grinning. 'The shack has been deserted since then.' He looked at me, a very serious demeanor on his face, and continued, 'The body was taken back to Mexico, some place close to Saltillo, I think. I had just started working for Rancho Casa Redondo when all this happened.'

"'There was an old man there…' I insisted.

"'The *caporal* shrugged and added, 'Maybe a *mojado* took up residence there. It is a big ranch and we can't keep an eye on everything. I guess I'll have to ride by there later, if I have time.'"

"The *caporal* didn't seem too eager," Alex added thoughtfully, "so on my way back I stopped by the shack to check on the old man. You can guess what I found."

I knew Alex so well that I guessed correctly, "The place was now abandoned, like the *caporal* said."

Alex frowned, "More than that." He furrowed his brow, searching for exactly the right words. "It was . . . completely devoid of human presence. The fireplace that had glowed so brightly earlier with mesquite embers was now not only stone cold, it was clean. I mean *clean*. The ashes completely swept out. There was nothing, *nada*, to indicate that anyone had been there in years."

Earlier, Héctor Villarreal, another operator, had come in for coffee and stayed to hear Alex tell his story. Now laughing he interrupted, "Well, Alex, I guess you supped with a ghost, ha, ha!"

"Nah," I interjected with a wiry grin, "not a ghost."

Héctor excitedly insisted, "But the *caporal* told Alex that the man had been dead for a long time. I don't think that the *caporal* would lie about something like that."

"I don't think that he lied, Héctor." Then I glanced at Alex and said, "I believe that the old man had been dead for some time. Alex, do you remember how the church is always hosting fund-raisers? Didn't the church have a fund-raiser to return the body of a cowboy found dead at some ranch to Mexico? Wasn't it to Saltillo?"

A flash of recognition washed across Alex's face. "I think so, but . . ."

I finished for Alex. "We were just kids in grade school when that happened."

Alex sat down hard in the black office chair, a very troubled expression crossing his face, "I wasn't even driving," he managed to say, "when that old cowboy died."

I nodded saying, "And yet, one does not break bread and have coffee with a ghost, so the old man must have been very much alive when you came knocking on his door—"

"Whoa," Héctor interrupted, now thoroughly confused, "was the old-timer dead or alive?"

"*That,* my friends, is the sixty-four-dollar question." I turned to Alex and asked, "Did you say that this incident occurred during the summer?"

"In fact it did, a right hot day, too."

"Makes perfect sense," I added.

Now both of my friends looked at me completely bewildered. I waved at them to assure them that I had not taken leave of my senses.

"I have a friend," I continued, "a man of science, who tells me that space and time are simply a continuum of the same thing. To grasp such an abstraction you have to change your thinking a little bit. It helps if you consider that earth, rain, wind, and fire are four primal elements possessing properties unique to each."

"Earth?" Héctor chuckled, "I don't know about earth, but Rain, Wind, and Fire is an old rock band!"

I smiled at Héctor's joke and continued, "Water and ice, although possessing vastly different properties, are really the same element. Cold is the only reason that we experience ordinary water as ice, or snow, or slush. And the only reason that we experience ordinary space as something other than space, in this case *time*, is because the gravitational force of the earth actually curves space. That curvature (or the process of having to constantly muddle through it) we experience as time."

"So what does that have to do with ghosts?" Héctor inquired.

I motioned for Héctor to be patient a moment longer. "If an old, horse-drawn wagon would happen to roll over a glass bottle with one of its wheels, what would happen?"

Alex arched an eyebrow and said, "I expect that the bottle would shatter. Those old wagon wheels were lined with steel."

"Years ago, when I was a kid, my father showed me an old glass bottle, you know the kind, the ones *tequileros* used to smuggle booze in during the Prohibition. It was flattened."

Héctor looked at Alex and asked, "How do you flatten a glass bottle?"

"My father," I continued, "had rolled over that bottle with his wagon wheel one hot summer day. When he didn't hear the bottle shatter, he stopped and retrieved it. It was completely flattened in the middle. We figured it had something to do with lying in the sun all day. In other words, extreme climatic conditions."

"That is very interesting," Héctor said impatiently, "but what does it have to do with ghosts?" He pulled his baseball cap off and crossed his arms nervously. "We were talking about ghosts."

"I believe that extreme climatic conditions can somehow warp the elements, as that bottle was flattened rather than shattered. Perhaps such extreme conditions can even alter that curvature that we call time."

Héctor shook his head impatiently and gave me a puzzled look. "I still don't get it. What does space, time, climatic conditions, *and* a flattened tequila bottle have to do with ghosts?"

"Héctor," I insistently asked, "when is a ghost not a ghost?"

Héctor and Alex looked at each other, then answered simultaneously, "When he's not dead."

I looked Alex square in the eyes. "You were very lucky, my friend. Thousands of people disappear each year." Here I snapped my fingers for emphasis. "Just vanish off the face of the earth. They are never seen or heard from again. What if they slip through time—"

Alex raised an eyebrow, "You mean I could have become . . ." He looked around as if searching for exactly the right word, "*stranded* in the old man's time?"

I smiled at my friends to ease the tension. It can be difficult when one first realizes that we live in a whimsical universe where the wrong fork in the road can lead to . . . *eternity*.

I took another sip of coffee and settled down in a chair myself. "You must have entered a time warp of some kind, momentarily visiting a place and period in time when the old man was still alive and well, preparing bread and coffee and quite anxious for some good conversation with one of his fellows."

As an afterthought I added, "I am glad that it was you and not me."

"Why?" Alex asked, "you're pretty good at talking. I'm sure that the old man would have enjoyed your company."

"That's the problem," I smiled. "I talk too much." I glimpsed around briefly to see if anyone disagreed. No one did. Frowning I added, "I certainly would have stayed too long and surely would have become trapped in the old man's time."

Alex and Héctor quietly nodded.

Thinking about it, I suddenly shivered. "Let's not dwell on it," I suggested, furrowing my brow, "after all, such an anomaly can occur but once in a lifetime to any one person."

Then I grinned and added, "It must be like winning the lottery. The odds have to be astronomical."

Alex smiled and said, "I think I would prefer to win the lottery."

The Little Girl Who Could See Death

Since people of Mexican heritage frequently portray the Grim Reaper as a woman, it should come as no surprise that Melly Rodríguez also referred to Death in the feminine gender. Melly was merely a seven-year-old in 1940 when she first glimpsed the Grim Reaper in her home in the lower Rio Grande Valley of Texas. Her neighbors believed that Melly possessed prophetic vision. Others said that she was a witch. "That little Rodríguez girl," they whispered nervously, "can strike you dead with her stare."

"I saw *la muerte* and for this I was severely beaten by my mother. I do not know why I see such things. It is not something that one asks for, to see Death." Melly Rodríguez, now sixty-seven years old, closed her eyes momentarily as if the memory still brought her pain.

"It is no easy thing to speak the truth," Melly continued, "when one can see Death calling on his *prójimo*—neighbor."

51

Melly went on to relate, in her own words, about the first time she spied Death's face in one of her neighbors: "A pregnant woman came to see my mother, who was a part-time seamstress, about a dress she was sewing. The woman had her little daughter with her, a beautiful little girl with long, wavy brown hair. 'How long,' my mother asked the pregnant lady, 'before the blessed event?' 'Another two weeks,' the lady replied. Then my mother turned to the little girl and said, *'En dos semanas te tumba la burra.'* That was a nonsensical expression meaning that the little princess is about to be dethroned by the new arrival.

"It was then, at that very moment, that I saw Death in the precious little girl's physiognomy. 'She will never know the baby,' I said with a child's simplicity, 'for tomorrow at three, this little girl will die.'

"Horrified my mother shouted at me, 'Shut up, Melly!' But I had spoken what I had seen, and by three-thirty the following afternoon, the little girl was dead.

"My mother beat me senseless. I could not cry. I have never been able to cry. As if infuriated by my lack of tears, my mother beat me even more. Through my pain and sorrow I could hear Death's wicked cackle.

"The neighbors wanted to lynch me. 'That Rodríguez girl is a witch,' the people cried, 'she killed her neighbor's daughter.' But I did not kill her. It was perhaps her fate to die at that time. I only spoke the truth of what I saw. Because of this, my parents had to smuggle me out of the house, to a place of hiding I will not name. It was a community some distance away where the incident was not known. Some two months later my parents relocated there.

"I was still seven the next time that I saw *la muerte*. I was helping prepare wax flowers for the impending funeral of an elderly man called Tata Choy. He was ninety-one years old, and had been in Death's grip for fifteen days.

"A lady by the name of Berthabe was there also. She was a beautiful young woman who had been married to Agustín for some six months. Agustín was what today would be called a security guard. He was hired out to keep peace at the weekend dances.

"Agustín then came by to kiss his beautiful wife good-bye, as he was scheduled to guard a dance that very evening. He chatted with his wife and the ladies for a few minutes, then he put on his gun belt to leave. As an afterthought Agustín mentioned before departing, 'Oh, by the way, I went by to see Tata Choy; I am afraid he will not live through the night.' 'It is you,' said I, 'who will not live through the night.'

"My mother was enraged, 'Shut up, child!' she screamed. "Agustín just smiled and told my mother not to reprimand me. 'She is only a child, Mrs. Rodríguez.' He walked up to me and gently caressed my hair. 'What does she know?'

"We were still working on the wax flowers when a messenger came by to inform Berthabe that her husband had been killed at the dance by *una bala perdida*—a stray bullet. In an instant my mother was all over me, to beat me senseless once again. She did not understand that this was a gift that I possessed. It was Berthabe herself that stopped my mother, staying her hand. Berthabe was surprisingly calm. 'Mrs. Rodríguez,' she said with conviction, 'do not beat this child. Do not punish her in any way. Can you not see that this child is gifted? Had my husband heeded her warning, he perhaps would have lived to see another day.'"

Belia

Rumors of creatures known as witches have been heard since the dawn of civilization. From the witch doctors of the Dark Continent to the crones of Salem, from the Good Witch of the East to the witches of Eastwick, witches have always made their presence known wherever civilization has taken a foothold.

"Witches are real," my older brother Eliazar would say, "at least Grandfather Apolonio believed that they were real. Since before you were born he would tell us of the days when he worked for a General Rodríguez . . ."

"In those days I worked for a General Rodríguez, close to Río Bravo, Tamaulipas," Grandpa Apolonio began. "We were clearing brush, clearing the right-of-way that came to be known as 102. Each morning I would start up my old tractor, its two big bucket-sized cylinders going boom-clunk, boom-clunk, boom-clunk, as I warmed it up. Then boom-clunk, boom-boom-boom-clunk, boom-boom-boom, as I made my way through the brush to the place where we were working. This was some five or six years before I married your grandmother.

"Each morning I would pass a clearing in the brush that had a little *jacal*—a crude shack made of earth and rough timber, *leña* really. The yard was kept up and someone was maintaining a small garden there.

"One morning I noticed a young lady tending the garden. Sitting on my old tractor I thought to myself that she was quite attractive. The following day, to my surprise, when I passed the *jacal* the young lady smiled and waved at me. Overcoming my surprise I managed to wave back, telling myself not to make too much of it. This morning is so beautiful and perfect, I rationalized, that everyone is in a fine mood and feeling friendly. Well, the following week, to my delight, the young lady started blowing kisses at me as I drove by. Embarrassed I simply waved to her and continued on my way. It was some three days later that I gathered up enough courage to stop by the girl's house. My pretext for stopping was to ask for a glass of water.

"From a closer distance, the girl was even more beautiful. In fact, I have not known a more beautiful woman. Her face reminded me of the image of Our Lady of Guadalupe. I learned that her name was Belia and that she lived alone. Belia was perhaps a year or two older than I, but we got along splendidly, and I soon found myself making excuses to stop to converse with her on my way to and from work.

"It seems that Belia was always working in her garden. She grew vegetables, chili peppers, beans, onions, tomatoes, as well as herbs and spices. One day Belia invited me in. Her house was simple but well kept and clean. On the rough walls dull yellow gourds were hung, as well as green, red, and yellow dried sweet peppers, and strands of garlic. The interior of the *jacal* smelled of damp earth, mingled with the fragrance of wildflowers, herbs, and spices. The interior was a combination kitchen, living room, and bedroom. Outhouses were the norm then, so I wondered about the single room in the back, separated from the rest of the *jacal* by a white sheet. I supposed that that was where Belia bathed, of course I didn't go back to *that* room.

"Belia told me, to my delight, that I was welcome to stop and visit with her anytime. However, under no circumstances was I to call on her on Tuesdays or Fridays. She offered no explanation, but counting myself fortunate to be on friendly terms with such a beautiful young woman, I did not question her provisos.

"I continued seeing Belia almost daily, spending more and more time by her side. My friends started missing me and asked what I was doing with all my free time.

"Spellbound, I related my good fortune to my closest friends, who cynically pointed out that this Belia was probably entertaining some other gentleman friend on Tuesdays and Fridays.

"'Undoubtedly,' they said, 'if she is as beautiful as you describe, then she must be seeing the wealthiest man in town. Don Alberto has much *plata*—silver and power. He can afford to keep such a beautiful *muñeca* hidden away from his *mujer*. You know that all that land belongs to Don Alberto, therefore the woman surely must be his as well.

"I was speechless. Indeed, the land did belong to Don Alberto, but what about the woman?"

"'Apolonio,' my friends continued, 'it is better that you stop seeing her before you get hurt. You are better off spending your free time with your *compadres*.'

"The thorn of jealousy pricked at my heart. The following day was Tuesday, and I stared at Belia's *jacal* on my way to work. Belia was nowhere to be seen. Somehow I made it through the workday. Driving back late that evening, with the poison of jealousy in my heart, I made my mind up to spy on Belia.

"I parked my tractor some distance from her *jacal*, far enough away that I knew she would not hear me coming. Then I carefully made my way through the thicket, to the brush line where her yard began.

"Belia was outside tending her garden. I looked all around but could see no other person. As the sun was going down, Belia stopped her toil and went inside her *jacal*, securing the door behind her.

"It was almost completely dark outside when I noticed a light inside the *jacal*. Belia had lighted a lamp. As quietly as I could, I snuck up to her *jacal* and walked around until I found a crack in the *leña* that afforded me a fair view of the inside. With my face pressed to the crack, the pungent odor of damp earth, herbs, and spices that permeated the interior bled through, tickling my nostrils. To my great relief, Belia appeared to be alone.

"I observed as she tidied up around her house. I was

feeling remorseful for allowing jealousy to make me question Belia's integrity. Perhaps she simply needed those two days to keep up with her chores and there was no nefarious reason for asking me to stay away on Tuesdays and Fridays. Just then I noticed Belia walk up to her bed, kneel down, and reach for something underneath. She withdrew a jar that appeared to be filled with a greasy ointment. With the jar in her hand she walked to the back room, the one separated from the rest of the house by the sheet. Belia parted the sheet, and believing herself to be alone and unobserved, did not bother to draw the sheet behind her.

"I was surprised to see a large, cast-iron kettle right in the middle of that room, where I had expected a bathtub. Belia then proceeded to bathe in that kettle.

"When she finished bathing, she dried off and proceeded to anoint her knuckles, toes, and all the joints of her body with the greasy substance in the jar. Belia then took a white robe from her bed and put it on. She grabbed a kerosene lantern and even though there was adequate lighting inside her *jacal*, she lit the lantern and held it up, adjusting the wick.

"With the lantern in her hand she walked to a corner of her house and took a broom. Then Belia straddled the broom sidesaddle, closed her big, beautiful brown eyes, and said, '*Ni con Dios, ni con la Santa Virgen María*—Not with God, nor with the Blessed Virgin Mary.'

"The front door blew open and a great gust of wind seemed to fill the *jacal*. It was a bitter cold wind that chilled me to the marrow, causing me to recoil from the crack in the wall. Now the *jacal* was engulfed in darkness, so I ran around to the front. Up in the air, hovering at tree-top level, I spied a light that could have been that of a kerosene lantern, if the lantern had wings and could fly.

"I was dumbstruck. Belia was nowhere to be seen. I struck a match and I called her name with a raspy voice. I ventured inside her *jacal*. There on the table was the table lamp. I quickly lit it and adjusted the wick, filling the *jacal* with light. 'Belia,' I called, 'Belia . . .' but there was no reply.

"I made my way to the back room and observed that the black kettle was indeed filled with water. The jar was on the floor by the kettle. I took the jar in my hand and stared at the mysterious ointment. Then on impulse I entered the kettle, quickly bathing. Imitating Belia, I dried off and anointed myself with the greasy ointment. I found another broom. Determined to follow Belia and learn her secret, I straddled the broom not concerned that I didn't have a kerosene lantern to light my way.

"I could not, I simply could not bring myself to repeat the phrase Belia had uttered before she disappeared. I tried, *'Con Dios, y con la Santa Virgen María*—With God, and with the Blessed Virgin Mary,' but the chant was wrong, or the broom was not intended for flight.

"Desperately, I searched outside for Belia. I even looked in the outhouse, but she was gone. I must have fallen asleep by the brush line, when a light startled me. How long had I slept? It was Belia returning to her *jacal*. I rushed to the door that she had not bothered to close. From the door I watched in astonishment as Belia removed her robe and dropped into the kettle. She quickly washed off the greasy ointment and withdrew from the kettle. Without bothering to dry off or change clothing, she went to her bed and dropped like a log. A moment later I bolstered my courage and ventured in.

"'Belia,' I called her name loudly, 'Belia!' but she was sound asleep. I shook her, but she seemed to be in a trance. She did not even stir.

"I walked to the back room intending to wash the ointment from my own body. To my astonishment, the water in the kettle was at a roiling boil with no fire to heat it!

"I covered Belia with a sheet and left her *jacal*, closing the door behind me. I didn't think she could be in any danger, as now I was sure that she was a *bruja*—a witch; I had more to fear from her than she from any man. I fled, as quickly as I could, stopping only at the nearest canal to wash off the ointment.

"I stopped working for General Rodíguez, not bothering to even collect my final wages. I simply did not want to have to drive by Belia's house. In fact, I never went by Belia's *jacal* again, nor did I look or ask for her. Don Alberto, if he was seeing her, was more than welcome to have her as far as I was concerned."

"That is a very interesting story, Eliazar. Do you suppose it was true?"

Eliazar shrugged his shoulders, and then staring into the distance said, "Grandpa said it was true." Then he smiled whimsically and added, "Who knows?"

The Year of the Witch

Oscar García was only ten years old in 1959, when he was terrorized by a bona fide, lantern-carrying, broom-riding witch. "I did not actually see a broom," Oscar says prosaically, "but she was carrying an old kerosene lantern. Now. I am familiar with those old lanterns. Today we call them hurricane lanterns and we fuel them with lamp oil or citronella. In those days the men used them at night when they irrigated the farm fields by hand. My family and I were Tex-Mex migrant farm workers from *el valle del* Río Grande."

The thing that frightened my sister and I that night in 1959 may not have been riding a broom, but she did fly, glide, and hover. I say thing, but I should say creature. I mean the term in the sense that it was some kind of living, breathing entity capable of acting deliberately and perhaps even maliciously. Now what kind of creature employs the use of tools or implements? A lantern certainly is a tool or an implement. It must be fueled, it must be lit, and the wick must be adjusted. It takes more than simple dexterity to accomplish these ends; it takes intelligence, purpose, and will beyond that given to the baser creatures of the planet.

We left the city of Pharr in the lower Rio Grande Valley of Texas in a caravan bound for the State of Wisconsin to labor in the fields. These were farm fields where our family would work hard, shedding sweat and at times even tears, to make an honest living and a better life for all of us. Six hours later our caravan, plagued by car problems, stopped in Goliad, Texas. The people in charge of the caravan decided that we should spend the night just outside the city in a roadside park.

My sister and I were alone in one of the cars. We were supposed to be sleeping but, excited by the fact that we were journeying to *el norte*, sleep eluded us. We were wide awake, talking about things that children talk about late at night when they are all alone—our plans for the future. My sister would marry Prince Charming. I would grow up to be the greatest sports figure ever. Our reverie was suddenly interrupted by a flash of light that moved silently across the night sky. My sister exclaimed, "Look, Oscar, a shooting star!"

"Let's make a wish!" I suggested.

We giggled excitedly as we contemplated a wish upon this very special shooting star, which was surprisingly not streaking across the heavens, burning out before we had time to even make a proper wish. This shooting star was more accommodating. It moved slowly, in an almost surrealistic manner, across the night sky. Abruptly, our giggles were stifled as we observed that this shooting star now came to rest upon the limbs of a great tree by the very roadside park where we camped.

More curious than afraid, we contemplated this strange sight, wondering what it could be. The light, for that is what it was, had an odd rocking motion to it. Staring intently at it we soon discerned that the light was that of an old kerosene lantern.

Now we could see a hand holding the lantern, and as it moved, we could see different body parts. A woman dressed in black and white rags perched on the tree, holding the lantern.

Suddenly, the woman descended from the tree and hovered, somehow suspended in midair, about another car in the caravan. She peered inside the car, then moved to yet another vehicle. Quietly, we watched as the woman glided, almost floating, from car to car.

The woman even visited all the people asleep in their sleeping bags on the cold, hard ground. No one stirred. What was her purpose? Through its mere presence, silence, and mysterious means of locomotion, this dark and ominous creature invoked feelings of dread and impending doom.

The air grew heavy and our breath became shallow, for now the creature floated toward *our* car. Time ceased. Quickly we buried our faces in the seat of the car, feigning sleep. We sensed the dark presence that electrified the atmosphere, raising gooseflesh and making our spines tingle with terror.

From the nearby highway we could hear the sound of a big truck rumbling in the night, rapidly approaching. When we ventured to look, the woman had retreated to the tree, only to return after the eighteen-wheeler zoomed by. Soon it became apparent to us that either the lights or the noise from the trailers, which were passing quite frequently now, were making the creature retreat to the tree.

"Oscar," my sister whispered, "there comes another trailer. *La bruja* is going to go back to the tree. As soon as she does, *'manito*, run as quickly as you can. Go get Papá. Bring him back, he'll know what to do."

As soon as I cracked the car door a bit, the witch swooped down upon our car in a flash. I quickly slammed the door shut and jumped over into the front seat where my sister and I cowered on the floorboard shielding our faces with our little arms.

The sound the witch made was horrible. It was not unlike that of a huge, hissing snake, but it also seemed to be . . . cracking something in its mouth. It sounded like when one crunches down on a mouth full of corn nuts and hisses, all at the same time.

Thankfully, another eighteen-wheeler shot by. This scene, however, replayed itself until close to daybreak, when the witch finally retreated the way she had come into the roadside park from the sky.

Neither my sister nor I could bring ourselves to relate

what happened that night to our parents. With the break of dawn came the mundane, everyday worries and problems that forever accompany the poor, itinerate laborer. We kept our terror to ourselves. Our parents had enough to worry about.

We continued our journey to Wisconsin. We made several stops because every so often, another car would break down, and in Wisconsin, serious disagreements occurred with the field man who was in charge of the work detail. Near destitution, cold, and hungry, we were aided by workers from an all-white migrant camp. They offered us work and provided food, blankets, and friendship.

Months later, we lost our Papá to stomach cancer, a malady we were not even aware he had. Although we did make good friends along the way, it was a year of change for us, a year my sister and I will forever remember as The Year of the Witch.

Last Is Not So Bad

One deer season during December of '79, some friends and I were hunting whitetail deer in Duval County, Texas. The other hunters, Daniel, J. J., and Martin, left the cabin well before daybreak. I was the last hunter to leave.

As I vacated the cabin I checked the thermometer that J. J., Javier José, had mounted by the front door away from the wind. He was meticulous about placing the thermometer away from the wind. "We want to know the atmospheric temperature," he would say, "not the windchill factor."

In that dark December morning, the temperature was exactly 32 degrees Fahrenheit, the freezing point of water. I smiled and hurried off toward my deer blind with my deer rifle slung across my left shoulder. It promised to be a good day to hunt deer. All night long a dense cloud cover had hidden the moon and stars; seasoned deer hunters knew that when deer are unable to feed by the light of the moon, they will be out at first light foraging for food. The cold weather forced game to move around in order to generate body heat, increasing the hunter's chance of sighting a choice deer to shoot.

The cold, clammy morning certainly gave credence to the truism that it's always darkest just before dawn, and soon I regretted having forgotten my flashlight in the cabin. I was not one to fear the dark, and wanting to be in my shooting blind before daybreak, I trudged on, following an old path.

At a point about a quarter of a mile from my blind, I stopped. *Danger*. Something indefinable lurked there in the dark on the side of the path, just a step away. It was silently waiting. I waited five minutes, then ten. I grew impatient, but something kept me rooted to the ground. Although it was still too dark to see, I stared intently at the spot on the side of the path and decided that there was no earthly reason why I shouldn't just keep going. Yet each time that I attempted another step I heard a voice inside commanding me not to take one more step.

The window of opportunity to be in my shooting blind before daybreak was closing rapidly. Even if I hurried I would not make it, so I resigned myself to wait until I could see what danger lurked there on the side further into the trail. Reasoning that nothing harmful could be there, I felt very foolish. Then I finally saw it and I was thankful I waited. As the first few rays of daylight filtered through the gray, overcast sky chasing the darkness away, I identified the unseen threat and my blood ran cold.

Some people claim that they can smell danger. I make no such claim. It was not fear that kept me rooted to my place, nor reason. Had I been fearful I would have backtracked to the cabin and slept in, making some lame excuse for not hunting that morning. In fact, I had been quite anxious to reach my shooting blind before daybreak, and logic had urged me that nothing impeded my goal, but something kept me from taking another step. As I stood there watching it, I was astonished. It should not be there. It appeared hungry, ravenous. It was neither the largest nor the smallest one I had ever seen, but it was large enough to kill with a single bite. It was a western diamondback rattlesnake, with a head as big as my fist, a girth as big around as my forearm, and a forked tongue that flicked silently in and out.

Quickly I dispatched the snake with a pistol that I carried for such an emergency. In its death throes it bit a rock almost as large as its own head. I watched in awe as the rock became saturated with deadly venom, a clear, thick slimy excretion about the color and consistency of egg white.

Knowing that the snake had spent all its venom and that it was now dead, I reached down and grabbed the snake by the tail. I judged its weight to be about six pounds, and on its rattler I counted sixteen beads. Rattlesnakes shed their skin as they grow, and in a good year a healthy snake may experience several growth spurts. The sixteen beads on this snake did not necessarily make it sixteen years old. Many old-timers said one bead on the tail of a rattlesnake equals one year of life, but rattlesnakes added a bead to their tail each time that they shed their skin.

Old-timers also said, "*Si quieres que llueva, halla una víbora de cascabel y mátala. Luego cuélgala de una cerca de alambre de púas y dentro de uno o dos días lloverá*—If you want it to rain, find a rattlesnake and kill it. Then hang it over a barbed-wire fence; rain will come for sure within a day or two." In South Texas there was never enough rain, so I hurled the snake over a barbed-wire fence, noticing that both ends came close to touching the ground. Nearly six feet long, I thought, as I proceeded to my shooting blind, realizing that my three pistol shots had probably spooked off all nearby game.

When evening came and all the hunters were back in the cabin, no one reported even seeing any game, much less shooting anything. My friends chided me for missing my target, as the meat locker was still empty and everyone had heard three shots coming from the direction of my blind.

"Think about it," I said to my friends, "those three shots you heard were not rifle shots."

"Come to think of it," J. J. replied, "they did sound like pistol shots. What did you shoot at, a coyote?"

"I shot a rattlesnake."

Simultaneously everybody in the cabin broke out laughing. Daniel admonished, "Now we know you're lying! You missed three shots at a big ol' buck and you won't admit it."

"I didn't see a deer, Dan, much less shoot at one—"

"Everyone here knows," Daniel insisted, "that snakes are cold blooded. They don't come out during cold weather. They hibernate. The temperature has been right at freezing all day long; you couldn't have shot a snake. You need to make up a better excuse than that one!"

"In the morning," I countered, "if the coyotes don't find it and eat it during the night, I'll show you guys the snake."

The following morning was bright and sunny and considerably warmer than the day before. The cloud cover was gone. It had rained all night long. We piled into Daniel's pickup and drove to the place where I had shot the rattlesnake. There was the snake, still draped across the barbed-wire fence, all five-feet-eight-inches and sixteen rattler beads of it. Daniel walked up to it and grabbed it around the midsection. Suddenly, the snake jerked spasmodically in his hand. My friend instantly leaped into the bed of his truck in a single bound.

"You're a lousy shot," he yelled at me, "the snake is still alive!"

Suppressing my laughter I managed to say, "It's dead all right; remember, snakes are cold blooded. It was freezing all last night. The cold kept it fresh. What you felt was just a muscle spasm." Then I cracked up laughing.

J. J. nonchalantly asked, "You want the hide or rattler?"

"I've seen enough rattlers to last a lifetime," I replied. "You can keep the hide and rattler if you want them."

Although no one shot a deer that weekend, everyone came out a winner. J. J. took the snake hide to make a belt and his little brother Martín took the rattler for his hatband. The coyotes got a meal they didn't have to fight for, and Daniel the rancher got his rain.

I profited most of all. I didn't get a snakebite that day and I ended up being the last one to laugh. Sometimes last is not so bad. . . .

The Shape-shifting Jackass

Higinio Hernández, Doña Tiburcia's brother-in-law, owned a cornfield that was approximately half-a-mile wide and four miles long. Enrique Guzmán, Higinio's neighbor, owned a jackass that loved to jump fences to graze on Higinio's corn.

Enrique, eager to be a good neighbor, constantly drove the jackass back. Each night, however, the jackass would jump the fence and be back in Higinio Hernández's cornfield.

Enrique owned a field some two miles away that seemed to produce nothing but rocks. The field was bare and unused. Enrique reasoned that the jackass should be taught a lesson by being left alone in that barren field for a while.

Perhaps, Enrique thought, the jackass will learn to respect fences and appreciate being where grass, rather than rocks, grows. Enrique hired Pancho Mireles to lasso the jackass and bind its front legs. Pancho, however, was not about to put up with the antics of a stubborn, cantankerous jackass for the two-mile drive to the barren field.

"Why don't you give that task," Pancho suggested, "to one of the *chamacos*—boys?"

Juan Rodríguez was only thirteen years old then, but he was a strong, obedient, and dependable worker.

"Juan," Enrique called, "I have a job for you to do."

"*Sí, Señor Enrique*," Juan all but stood at attention awaiting his orders from *el patrón*.

"You know where my field of rocks is, Juan?"

"*Sí, Señor*, the place where nothing grows."

Enrique smiled. The boy was sharp. "I will pay you two silver *pesos* to lead that cantankerous jackass," Enrique pointed at the hapless beast, "by force if necessary, to that barren field. Leave him there, Juan. Tie his front legs so that he cannot escape. There he will learn to appreciate having grass to eat, and he will stop stealing my neighbor's corn."

"*Como usted mande, patrón*—as you have ordered, boss," Juan replied, hurrying toward the jackass.

"And Juan," Enrique called, "take this horsewhip with you, if you have to, do not hesitate to make use of it."

Juan struggled with the jackass most of that afternoon. With its front legs tied, the jackass had to hobble along, braying in protest the forced, two-mile trek to its new home. When the jackass stopped too long, Juan would administer a sharp slap with the horsewhip to urge it on.

Finally the barren field came into view. Juan pushed the jackass along, stopping only to open the gate to let it in.

Juan wiped the sweat from his brow as he closed the

gate behind him. He would lead the jackass in a little further into the field, and then his task would be done. It was now that Juan noticed, to his great dismay, that the rope binding the jackass's front legs had flayed the hide from its feet. Enough, Juan thought, I shall leave the poor jackass here by the gate. Juan had dropped Señor Enrique's horsewhip. Now he looked down to retrieve it. When Juan looked up again, the biggest coyote he had ever seen was standing there, a low growl issuing from deep within its throat.

Juan looked for the jackass, hoping to put the jackass between him and the menacing canine. The jackass had vanished. In its place was what could only be, from its sheer size, a lobo. It was of monstrous proportions, very skinny, hunched back, and very hairy, with the biggest teeth Juan had ever seen. It growled deeply, menacingly as it inched toward Juan.

Juan searched for the horsewhip. It would be something to use to keep the beast at bay until help came along. Suddenly, Juan caught a glimpse of the horsewhip on the ground. He dived for it, feeling the wolf's hot breath at his back. Juan grabbed the horsewhip and looked up again. The wolf was gone! In its place was the jackass, now peacefully nudging the rocks on the ground, seeking scraps of roots to munch on.

Juan believed that the jackass had changed itself into a wolf as punishment for mistreating it. Juan earned his two silver *pesos*, but he lost the use of his voice for three days.

Glossary of Spanish Words & Phrases

Agua con azúcar: Mexican folk remedy used to treat trauma.

Aquí: Here; here it is.

Bruja: Witch; a wicked or malicious woman.

Caballo: Horse.

Cabritos: Kid goats.

Caldo de pollo: Chicken soup or broth. Note: Pollo literally means "chick"; in Spanish the word "pollo" is always used when naming the entrée.

Caporal: Foreman; the chief cowboy working for a ranch.

Carranzista: Followers of Mexican President Venustiano Carranza (1859–1920), an opponent of Pancho Villa.

Chamaco/a: An informal term for boys or girls; one of the boys.

Chaparral: Low brush.

Compadres: Formally, the relationship a child's parents have with the persons who have sponsored that child in the Sacrament of Baptism or Confirmation. Informally, good friends.

Con Dios y con la Santa Virgen María: With God and with
the Blessed Virgin Mary.

Cuento: Tale; story or folk story.

Curandero/a: A person who specializes in folk medicine; a
healer.

Don: Title of respect for a man who has achieved a certain
dignity.

Doña: Feminine of "Don." A Don's wife.

El desierto muerto: Literally, the dead desert. Formerly the
name of a portion of present day South Texas when
Texas south of the Nueces River pertained to the Mexican state of Tamaulipas.

El norte: A way of saying "up north" in Spanish.

El patrón: The boss.

El Rancho: The name of the theater; literally, the ranch.

El valle: The Valley; a reference to the Rio Grande Valley
of Texas.

El viejito: Diminutive for "old man"; literally, the little old
man.

En ancas: A reference to the rider in back when riding tandem, particularly on horseback.

General: High military rank.

Gitanos: Gypsies.

Huisache: The sweet acacia tree common to South Texas.

Jacal: Hovel; stick house.

La Colonia el Gato: The name of a subdivision; literally,
"cat colony."

La gente de más antes: People of a bygone era; the old

folk; the wise old-timers.

La gente mayor: The older people worthy of respect.

La luz del llano: The light of the prairie. A spook light indigenous to a region of South Texas centering around Jim Hogg County.

La muerte: Death personified. In Mexican mythology, "death" is frequently personified as a woman, either comely and seductive or skeletal and horrible, sometimes both.

Las tías: Aunts.

Leña: Firewood; dry wood.

Los abuelos: The grandparents.

Los tíos: The uncles.

'manito: A contraction for "hermanito," little brother.

M'ijo: My son. A contraction for "mi hijo."

Macho: Of male gender; very masculine.

Maldita mujer: Cursed woman; malicious woman.

Mojado: A term of abuse for a person who has entered the country illegally by swimming across the Rio Grande River; a wetback.

Mujer: A woman; someone's wife.

Muñeca: A doll; a gorgeous woman.

Nada: Nothing.

Ni con Dios, ni con la Santa Virgen María: Not/nor with God, nor with the Blessed Virgin Mary.

Nopal: Cactus; prickly pear cactus.

Novelas: Soap operas.

Padrecito: Diminutive for father or priest.

Palo blanco: The netleaf hackberry tree common to South Texas.

Pan de campo: Bread prepared in a pan and cooked over a campfire; country bread.

Pesos: Standard monetary unit in Mexico similar to the U.S. dollar but of lesser value.

Plata: Silver. Hard money, silver coins especially silver pesos or silver dollars.

Que había quedado asustado: Permanently frightened or traumatized.

Quién sabe: A rhetorical question or an expression: "Who knows?"

Señorita: Miss; an unmarried woman of any age.

Tequilero: A bootlegger; a person who smuggled tequila from Mexico into the United States, particularly during the Prohibition.

Traigo a la muerte en ancas: A nonsensical expression similar to "with a monkey on your back," meaning that the Grim Reaper is riding tandem with someone on horseback and referring to the rider in the back.

Un rancho encantado: A haunted ranch.

Vaquero: A working cowboy.

Vaya con Dios: A layperson's blessing; may God be with you.

Yegua: A mare.

Additional Young Adult Titles

Mexican Ghost Tales of the Southwest
Alfred Avila, edited by Kat Avila
1994, Trade Paperback, ISBN 1-55885-107-0, $9.95

"These 21 Mexican folk tales . . . are uncommonly creepy. Short and punchy, these tales will be easy to book talk, and the relaxed, conversational tone of the text lends itself to reading and telling aloud." —*BOOKLIST*

Trino's Choice
Diane Gonzales Bertrand
1999, Trade Paperback, ISBN 1-55885-268-9, $9.95
Accelerated Reader Quiz #35007

When Rosca, an older teen with a vicious streak, invites Trino Olivares to start hanging out with his crowd, the younger boy doesn't know what to think. It's up to Trino to decide which choices will impress his friends, and which choices are the best for him.

Trino's Time
Diane Gonzales Bertrand
2001, Clothbound, ISBN 1-55885-316-2, $14.95
Trade Paperback, ISBN 1-55885-317-0, $9.95
Accelerated Reader Quiz #54653

In the sequel to the award-winning *Trino's Choice,* Trino finds himself even more alone. With the help of some friends and a Tejano hero that Trino discovers in history class, Trino chooses to take charge.

Orange Candy Slices and Other Secret Tales
Viola Canales
2001, Trade Paperback, ISBN 1-55885-332-4, $9.95

In this debut collection of coming-of-age stories, Canales introduces the reader to the cultural traditions of a border community: homage to the Virgin of Guadalupe, the day of the Three Magi, a carousel of unique saints and a flock of pink plastic flamingoes.

Lorenzo's Secret Mission
Rick and Lila Guzmán
2001, Trade Paperback, ISBN 1-55885-341-3, $9.95

Armed with a long knife, flint-lock musket, and his father's medical bag, fifteen-year-old Lorenzo Bannister joins a secret flatboat operation delivering much-needed supplies to George Washington's army. This action-packed historical novel for young people tells the story of Gibson's Lambs and the Spaniards, forgotten heroes of the American Revolution.

Lorenzo's Revolutionary Quest
Rick and Lila Guzmán
2003, Trade Paperback, ISBN 1-55885-392-8, $9.95

In this sequel to *Lorenzo's Secret Mission,* the intrepid young adventurer is back to fulfill his commitment to the American Revolution.

Spirits of the High Mesa
Floyd Martínez
1997, Trade Paperback, ISBN 1-55885-198-4, $9.95
Accelerated Reader Quiz #35010

"Although the sense of place is vivid on every page, the story is one that could be told about almost any part of rural America—the blessing and the curse of being opened to the world with the coming of electrification, roads and industry."   *—HOUSTON CHRONICLE*

... y no se lo tragó la tierra
Tomás Rivera
1996, Trade Paperback, ISBN 1-55885-151-8, $7.95
Accelerated Reader Quiz #20912

... y no se lo tragó la tierra, in the original Spanish, is Tomás Rivera's classic novel about a Mexican-American family's life as migrant workers during the 1950's, as seen through the eyes of a young boy.

Walking Stars
Victor Villaseñor
2003, Trade Paperback, ISBN 1-55885-394-4, $10.95
Accelerated Reader Quiz #35002

"These stories . . . are spellbinding and diverse. *Walking Stars* is an exquisite example of quality literature that helps explain diverse cultures and beliefs while unifying us all within the human family."   *—BOOKLIST*